The Adventures of James and The Undying Necklace

Chapter 1: Before the adventure

James, a ten-year-old boy, had powers! Superhero powers. He lay in his bed, playing with his action figures!

"IM GONNA GET YOU!" James shouted, imitating one of his action figures!

"No, you won't!"
"Haha!" said James, imitating the other doll!

As he was playing, he heard, a knock on the door outside.

His parents were out. They told him that they were going to the supermarket to get food and then they were going to pick their sister up and that if anyone knocks check out the window and see if they do a thumbs up. He parents said that the thumbs-up was the first signal! His sister was not home for a few days, so to hear that she was coming back, he was happy!

He looked out the window, and the man

stared at him with a
thumbs up!
He gulped, went down
and opened the door!

"Hello, boy," said the
man

"Hello, umm sir," said
James clutching his
action figure

"Your parents have
died" "They have left

you this letter," said
the man

"Wha-what" "They
have d-di-DIED!" "Give
me that letter! I need
to read what it said"
said James crying.

"Here," said the man

The letter was on a
special parchment!
It read;

Dear my sweet James,

I thought that I could keep this a secret, but the time has come! We have been hiding some secrets from you! Number 1 is that you have special powers! You have capabilities only some have like your sister, your mum and me!

Number 2 is that we were not going to get food and to pick up your sister! A renowned super villain kidnapped her! We are going to stop him, but we might die! Your sister might feel too!

Number 3 is that you are going to a particular school! A one where you can learn new special powers, and you can stay there during school time! If we do die, you will be living with your Aunt and if she marries someone else that person! Oh, and that person that gave you this letter is your teacher at your school!

I hope you understand!

Love from Dad

James jaw drooped! His sister was dead too!

"Umm sir," asked James

"Yes boy," said the man

"I'm kind of scared now" "Does that person want to kill me."

"Well I can't tell you;
you're too young! I can
tell you one thing
though: you are quite
famous in our special
world."

"What do you mean?
I'm popular!"

"Yep! That man tried
killing you, but he
couldn't! Your powers
were so out of control
that you knocked his

eye out! That is when he went to your sister, where he succeeded. You're known as the one who survived. Because of you, he can only see through one eye!"

"Serves him right for trying to kidnap me!"

"Well here is a letter from the headmaster of that school! Read the letter and then talk."

The man handed James the letter and read it;

Dear James,

You have been enrolled in the School of Superpowers! Since you are only ten (Like everyone else who joins), you will be starting in Year 1

Please find the enclosed list of items that you must buy from Scrubs;

A book of future readings by Jenifer Mozart

Beginners guide to all of the powers by James Enna

A cape

A unique umbrella
which you can use to
cast spells!

This is all you need for
now!

Yours sincerely,

Norman Trinity

James has thousands of questions, but he only asked one.

"Can you come with me to scrubs" "I don't know where it is."

"Of course! I am one of your teachers, anyway! But for now, you are coming with me to my home since you can't stay here, and your dad always told me how annoying your Aunt is" said the man.

"Oh, thank you! I hate their son" said James.

Chapter 2: The Preparation

James woke up thinking it was all a bad dream, but it was not! It woke up in the man's guest room! It was the cleanest room he had ever seen! No spiders, no dust; just shininess!

"Ahhh, you are awake! Perfect! Here are some bacon, eggs and toast."

"Umm, sir I forget to ask what your name is?"

"My name is professor David," said David

"Thank you, and I will keep that in mind."

"Eat up! Eat up! We don't want to be late for our journey to scrubs!"

"Oh, we are going today! Yay!"

Thirty minutes later, James comes dressed and ready!

"Wow, you look like Noil."

"What is a noil."

"Well, a noil is a person who has no powers."

After a bit of chatting, they packed

their bags and went outside!

"What vehicle are we going in?"

"This one. This car is particular so you might be a bit scared! This car can fly! No noil can see though! Only those who are our kind."

"Oh, that is quite nice."

They both hopped in looking quite happy!

Chapter 3: The Journey

During the journey, Professor David and James said nothing! They went for 20 minutes until James asked.

"Can noils see Scrubs?"

"Technically, no." said professor David

"They can only see an abandoned village and the is a sign which only they can see. The sign always reads"
DANGER! DO NOT ENTER! VERY DANGEROUS

"Woah, that's cool."

"I agree with you,"
said Professor David

A few minutes went by
as they talked about
what noils can see and
what they can't like
Scrubs or the School
of Special Powers.
Then Professor David
changed the subject.

"James look down
there, and you can see

scrubs," said Professor
David

"It's so big," said
James looking so
ecstatic

"Hold on tight! We are
landing!" said Professor
David

The car was as fast as
a high-speed train. It
just kept on going
down with no end to it.

"We are here,
James," said professor
David

"Woah," said James

"Okay, the plan is that
we first go to your
parent's lawyer and
get a slip that says
you inherited their
money, then we go to
the bank of Scrubs
and show them the

slip, they will then lead us to a special room where they will keep your money! You understand, right?" asked professor David who was trying to catch a breath.

"Yes sir," said James

"Good, follow me," said professor David

They walked into the building, and professor David started typing code on a keypad. He pressed the numbers 256390, and the machine started speaking.

"Welcome to Scrubs! Please state your name and your business with being with us."

"Hello, It is professor David, here with James Foster! We are here to go to the Lawyer of Mr and Mrs Foster and get the sheet of inheritance. Then we must buy school supplies!" answered Professor David.

"Please take these two badges and pin them

on your chest! Have a great time at Scrubs".

James was speechless; he had never seen anything so unusual in his life.

"James? James?" Repeated Professor David

"Oh yeah, sorry", said James feeling bad.

"We are here", said Professor David

Chapter 4: The Lawyer

The place looked like an abandoned home! The walls were covered with moss, and there were spiders everywhere! James looked like he was going to straight-up puke! But thankfully, he did not!

"Is-is that it?" Asked James while trembling

"Yep! There is no need to be scared. It is only like this because the owner is very elderly".

"So is the Lawyer elderly?" asked James

"Oh, no, no, no! The Lawyer is 39. That building is not his. It was some older person called Denis Cedric! No one would give him a building to start his business until your mum and dad went to him. He became so popular that he gave your mum and dad a job there!" answered Professor David.

"So, my parents worked there! That's cool. They never let me come to work because they always told me that it was too dangerous." responded James.

"They are right! Being a lawyer in our world is very dangerous! People get hurt every day! Little kids, big

kids even adults." said
Professor David.

James walked up to
the door and knocked.
No one responded.
James knocked on the
door once more.

"Who is it?" replied
the man

"Hello, it is Professor
David with James
Foster! We are here

to collect the inheritance note of Mr and Mrs Foster" answered Professor David.

"Come on in" replied the man.

"Hello, Mr Foster and Hello John" answered the man.

"Hello, Robert! Can we please have Mr

Foster's inheritance note!" asked Professor David.

"Of course! Just make sure he signs here and here" responded Robert.

After James had signed the form, they were given the inheritance slip.

"We will take off now.
Bye-bye!" said
Professor David.

"Take Care of him",
said Robert.

"I will." Responded
Professor David

Chapter 5: The Bank

There was a moment
of long silence until
James asked Professor
David a question.

'Professor, now that
we have the slip do,
we go to the bank and
claim the money?"
asked James

"Well, You have two
options, you can either
collect a whole lot of
locks now or later!"

Said, Professor David

"What are locks and also I will take some of it immediately and a bit later", said James

"Well, locks is our currency! Your parents were wealthy! They had more than 100,000 locks which are equivalent to 1,000,000 pounds! Quite a lot, you know" replied Professor David.

"Woah, my parents were that rich! No wonder how they bought me those action figures! I had one more in my collection, and they said that they would buy me it today, but know their d-d-dead." replied James tearfully

"Oh, don't get upset. We can buy the action figure if you want!" said Professor David trying to make James feel happy.

"Oh, wow, thank you! But why? I have never known who you are until yesterday. Why would you spend money for me?" asked James curiously.

"Well, I can't tell you yet. You're not the age that I imagined your father would tell allow you to know. Tell you what, I will tell you but in July when the School year ends! Deal?" said, professor David.

"Deal!" replied James

They did not speak for a while. James was

thinking about his new action figure while Professor David was considering whether he should tell him or not.

They walked for a reasonable amount of time until they reach the Bank of Scrubs. The bank was as large as three large mansions mushed together! James looked at the bank and thought Woah.

"Are you ready to go in, James?" asked Professor David.

"Yeah, I think so."

James opened the door to see a gorgeous bank! James thought they had gone to the wrong place, but he was wrong!

"Hello, welcome to the Bank of Scrubs! How may I help?" said the loud voice.

James heard someone say it, but he did know where they were.

"Hello, down here", repeated the loud voice.

"Harry these are gremlins", said Professor David in a hushed voice
"Hello there, I am Professor David with James Foster! We are here to enter room 863. We have an inheritance note!" said Professor David

"Of course, welcome Mr Foster. John, can I have a word?"

"Sure! James stays right here".

"Good Follow me!" Said the gremlin

As they walked away, James was dazzled by the bank. There were gremlins everywhere. Some are doing paperwork, some doing maths and some just walking around the place.

Meanwhile, the gremlin was asking Professor David many questions.

"So, the rumours are true! Mr and Mrs Foster have died!" asked the gremlin.

"And their daughter, yes", responded Professor David.

"WHAT?"

"We can talk about this later! Can we go to the room or not?"

"Yes, very well."

James was standing there waiting for than them to come. When they did, the gremlin asked them to follow him!

Chapter 6: Room 863

They walked for a while since room 863 was in the last row. When they did arrive, the gremlin was tugging Professor David's leg.

"Scan the inheritance note!" said the gremlin

"Idiots." said the gremlin in a hushed voice

Professor David took the slip out of his hand and placed on the scanner.

"Thank you for scanning! Your barcode is correct; you may enter!"

James pulled open the door, but the gremlin closed it.

"Before you enter were these" replied the gremlin.

The gremlin gave the two sunglasses. James didn't overthink until he opened the door. The room was so much gold the walls were gold too!

James has never seen so many gold coins! He looked shocked but puzzled since his parents always told him that they did not have much money, but he left thought and started touching all the gold.

"So, John, I understand you are responsible since you are his-"

Professor David stopped him mid-sentence.

"Shut your mouth! I have not told him yet!" said Professor David in a hushed voice

The gremlin responded with nothing but asked James questions.

"How much money do you want to takeout?" asked the Gremlin

"Ummm, maybe 5000, Nocks!"

"Okay, here is a bag of 5000 nocks

"Wow, that was quick!"

"Your parents sorted their money into

drawers," said
Professor David

"Bye-bye, it was nice
meeting you mist-"

Professor David had
stopped James mid-
sentence. He was
dragged outside where
the two said nothing.

Chapter 7: Books, Umbrellas, and capes

Professor David and James said nothing for their whole journey to Jalxes, the cape and umbrella store. They just kept on walking until they reached Jalxes.

James, without looking at Professor David, opened the door. The place was so loud until James entered.

"Are you not that boy who took Scrows' eye out?" said one kid.

"Are you that famous boy?" went another child.

Suddenly, All eyes were on James. James stood there like a statue. He did not know whether he should react to their comments or just carry on shopping! But before he could do anything, someone interrupted.

"So, this is Mr., I'm the best. Gosh, no wonder no one already likes you." Said the boy.

"Who are you, and what's your deal?" James asked

"I am the excellent most prestigious George Dartmouth! Listen here, I know more about your family then you will ever know. I know that your sister was expelled from this school and I know where your parents died. You may think that you know a lot about your family, but you're wrong. Have a great day!" replied George as he walked away.

James went up to Professor David. He thought to himself should I or should I not tell him what

George just told him.
In the end, he never
told him and just said

"I've got my stuff!"

"Good, come on, let's
go pay!" replied
Professor David.

Once they had paid,
they were back on the
streets! James had a
strong feeling in his
stomach where he

thought he should tell
Professor David what
George had said, but
he ignored the feeling
and carried on walking
to The Book store.

When they eventually
arrived at the store,
it was not as crowded
as Jaxles. No one was
there except James
and Professor David!
They looked through
the aisles of books

when they were
interrupted by a boy
named Max.

"Hey, is it your first
time at that school
and are you not that
you who knocked an
eye out from that
supervillain?" asked
max.

"Yes, and yes. Do you
want to be friends?"
James asked

"Sure!" replied Max

James left the store
with all his things,
happy that he has
made a friend but
confused about why his
sister was expelled.
He went to Professor
David's home, and
that was the first day
in the mighty,
compelling world.

Chapter 8: Two months later

"James, wake up! It's time for school. , shouted Professor David.

James awoke to hear Professor David's voice. It took him a few minutes to realise

he is going to a new school.
He was bursting with excitement and could not believe it. He went to the bathroom and brushed his teeth and had a shower.

He looked through his wardrobe and found the uniform they bought at Scrubs. He was smiling as he had never done before.

"James are you awake?" asked Professor David with an angry tone

"Yep, just putting my uniform on," replied James.

"Oh, all right." said Professor David in a more calming tone

James hurried downstairs and went into the kitchen where he had breakfast. He had bacon, eggs and toast with a bit of orange juice.

"Professor, how do I get to school?"

"Well, I give you some milk and put a little bit of a potion. When you drink it, you say the words Take me to the School of Superpowers. I will be coming with you since I am one of your teachers." replied the Professor

"Oh, okay. This seems cool."

"Well there is a lot in the superpower kingdom that you don't know about, and they

are cool. Let me show
you one. Put your hand
on your heart and say
Come out, oh, please
come out."

James did everything
David said, and when
he did it, a wolf came
out.

"See that. That is
your guardian whenever
you're in danger, do
that and the person

attacking you won't be able to go anywhere near you."

"Woah that is so cool."

Once Professor David had finished brewing the potion, he got two glasses of milk and put the potion in.

James chugged it all up and said the words.

Chapter 9: Section B Room 206

James was at school but in the wrong spot. He was teleported to Section B Room 206. This room was horrible. The room was filled powerful, magical beasts that could kill you in a minute. James luckily spawned in the safe zone; an area where the creatures can't enter.

He started to panic since he could not get out without dying. He started thinking of all the ways to go until he saw a necklace on the ground. It was shiny gold and had a pendant that looked like an action figure. James crept grabbed the

chain and ran back to
the safe area.

He looked at it and
saw an area where he
could place his thumb.
He put his thumb, and
it said

"YOU ARE NOW THE
RIGHTFUL OWNER OF
THIS UNDYING
NECKLACE. WITH
THIS YOU CANNOT
DIE. WEAR IT AND

SAY THE WORD
MAKE THY NECKLACE
INVISIBLE."

James knew what
everything the voice
said meant, and he did
exactly what the
necklace said. He got
out of the safety area
and left with his heart
beating.

Outside the door stood, Professor David.

"James, I have been looking all over for you! How did you get there?"

"The teleporter potion brought me here."

"All right, go to the assembly hall. There is lots of food in there."

"Yes, Professor."

Chapter 10: The Selection

James entered the assembly room with a wow look on his face. He saw large banners and for chairs with ghosts on top. He sat down and was next to Max.

They both smiled and played rock, paper scissors. Soon enough the headmaster, Norman Trinity stood up.

"Hello, Welcome first years and welcome back all other years. Today we will start with the selection ceremony, and then you will be given your timetable. Your house leaders, who are Professor Sedgemoor for Hawks, Professor Giffard for Agenes, Professor Joseph for Alexander and Professor Simon for Cecilia. Now when I call your name, sit on the yellow seat."

"James, please come up."

James stood up,
walked to the chair
and sat down.

"I don't want this kid
in my house. Move up!"
Said the Ghost

James then moved
along to the next seat.

"Sorry, not my house's
type."

James moved along again, where he got accepted.

"Nice kid, got a great future. HAWKS" shouted the Ghost

The whole room started clapping, especially the Hawks.

The same thing happened for max. He got accepted into

Hawks as well. Once
all the Yr1s were
sorted, they were
given their timetable
and were told to head
up to their house
room.

Chapter 11: The First Class

All the Hawks entered
the room in a beautiful

straight line with their
House Professor.

"Now can Yr 1 get in a
line and the rest of
the years please wait
for the other 3
Professors to come!"

"Follow me, Yr 1!"
shouted Professor
Sedgemoor

They all followed
Professor Sedgemoor

out and were very
quiet except James
and Max. They were
still jumping up around
happily since they were
both in Hawks.
They arrived outside a
door which said
"MAGICAL ROOM".

"Now, children in this
room is where we will
teach you a new spell.
"Now can I have all of
you enter in, and I will

teach you something
called fire breath!"

They all entered the
room, excited to learn
something new. Max
and James sat next to
Sana, who was also a
first year.

"Hi, do you want to be
friends?" Asked Maya

"Sure, I'm James, and
he is Ma-"

"Your James! The one
that hurt that villain
dude!?"

"Yep, that is me!"

"Settle down class!"
shouted the Professor

"Now, as I told you,
we are leaving fire
breath. This will help
when in a battle or
really anything, and as

the name suggests, you
will breathe fire. Now
take out your umbrella
and put it right at
your mouth and say
"Fire Breath!"

James did precisely
that while some others
were lit on fire.

"Now those of you who
have not lit themselves
on fire, please take a

deep breath in and then blow."

James did exactly that again and burned the table!

"Well done, James. If we practise on your control, you will be AMAZING at this!" Shouted the Professor. They all left the classroom for free period.

Chapter 12: Free Period

James left happily since his first-class went so well and that he made another new friend. Maya and Max were waiting for him at the bench.
They had snacks at the ready and were

easy to give hungry
James little snack.

"James over here!"
Shouted the Maya and
Max

James went dashing
down the pavement to
get to the bench
where they were
sitting. Maya and Max
gave James a can of
lemonade and crips.

They talked about
homework and where
they were from until
interrupted by George.

"Fancy seeing you
here. Thought you
would bail out of
coming here after
what I told you," said
George with an angry
tone

"Listen here, if you
wanna get attack

James you need to get through us."

"Yeah!"

James quietly crept to the back of George and put his and on his heart and said "Please come out oh, please come out". His wolf appeared and started tickle, George. George could not see the wolf, so he was confused and had a very nervous laugh.

"Uhhh.. what is going on?"

James had just whispered his plan to the others. They looked at George and laughed and turned their back at him.

Chapter 13:
Charms Class

"Yr 1, Please follow me to your charms class."

They followed the Professor into class. Everyone had just sat down, and the professor started her introduction.

"Charms are quite simple and except some of you have practised charms."

"Charms can take many forms, but the ones that are the most hardy and robust are the type we craft from the air. Charms are emotions, impulses; they are the lifeblood of magic."

"Today, we shall attempt to create a truth charm; this charm will compel the one it is cast upon to answer one question truthfully."

"It's quite a simple spell, as it's only one question. More advanced truth-telling charms are far more complex."

"The most advanced types are kept with the Leader of the Wizardry world for integration purposes. Anyway, to create this charm, you will need to craft it yourself from the emotions around you. Compel them to take form and mix them in the right order."

"We will use the crystals (that I will be handing out) to channel them; you will need to select crystals that are the primary colours. The primary colours are RED, BLUE AND YELLOW. You must select crystals of those colours to get the charm right."

"Do you know what you're doing?" asked the Professor.

'Yes, Professor!" shouted the class.

James had an idea, and it was not going to be beautiful. He was going to use the Truth Charm on George to find out more about his parents. He chucked the materials into the backpack, and I asked the teacher for a different one. The teacher asked no questions and just gave it to him.

James finished the class with a grin on his face, and he knew his plan was going to work.

Chapter 14: The Janitor's closet

James caught up with Maya and Max, and He had one big favour.

"Can you guys find me a room that no one uses or normally enters?"

"Oh, I know a room. The Janitors Closet" replied Max.

"Why do they even have a Janitor's closet? Can't they just clean the schools with magic?" asked James.

"Yeah, but I don't think they want us to get into the magic atmosphere too quickly."

"Oh well, do you know how to get there?"

"Yep! First Floor, Turn Right, walk another flight of stairs and then turn left," said Maya in a tongue-twister.

"Do you have a map or something?" asked James.

'Yeah, umm here. This will automatically change to the floor your own on its own."

"Cool, thanks. Catch you guys at lunch," shouted James as he dashed away.

He ran to the Hawks room and put money on the ground. Once he saw that George had contact with the money he was going to pull the money with his wand and lead him into the janitor's closet.

Slowly, but successfully he lured him in.

"Hey! Where am I?"

"Hello, George. It is time to lay my favourite game, Threaten the Student.

"What do you mean?" said George in a scared tone.

"You know what these are. They are the materials for the Truth Charm. Now I will make you tell me the TRUTH on why my parents died or why my sister was expelled! Now either tell me, or you're going to have to feel the Truth Charm."

"Oh, alright. Your sister was trying to

get into Section B
Room 206. She wanted
to get the Undying
necklace. If you wear
that necklace, you
cant die."
James felt something
in his stomach, but he
carried on listening to
what he was saying.

"Now, your parents
were lawyers and were
big in the magical
community and hated

my mum and dad. They committed many crimes, so yeah. My parents had a plan to lure them out and make the Villain dude not only kill your sister but your parents."

James was so angry. He was mad at his parents and Professor David.

"One more thing. Is Professor David related to my parents?" asked James.

"Umm, I have no comment on that."

"TELL ME NOW OR FEEL THE TRUTH CHARM!" Shouted James

"Okay, Professor David is your-."

He was stopped mid-sentence by an alarm that went off inside school.

"ATTENTION WONKERS HAVE ENTERED THE BUILDING! THEY ARE HERE FOR JAMES, FIRST YEAR, HAWKS. JAMES PLEASE

HIDE!" went the
microphone.

"Oh, no. Wonkers are
here," shouted George
in a frightful tone

"What are they?"
asked James

"They are snakes that
are the evil Villain. He
can transform himself
into a snake and
duplicate himself," said

George, who was very scared.

"What are we going to do?"

"Just stay here, and we will survive."

Hours went by until an announcement was made.

"Hello, students of
this excellent school. I
am known as the a
Villain, but let me tell
you a story that will
surprise you all.

"I was once born a
sweet little boy until I
was 16, where a
friend of mine showed
me the path of
becoming a villain in
this fine community.
Now, I have been on

the hunt for a boy
called James. This boy
DISRESPECTED me in
a whole new manner,
by poking my eye out.
But don't worry, I'm
wearing his father's
eye as a replacement."

James wanted to just
burst out crying, but
George helped him by
telling him that he
could die if he cries.

For four straight hours, nothing happened, until the rattling noises of the snake came closer to the closet. And the door was opened. James had a plan. He showed George the protection trick Professor David had taught him. Once they had that activated, they were going to use fire breath to blow

him away and try to
burn him.
  James also
remembered that he
could not die thanks to
the undying necklace.
The door creaked open
and "BANG" "BOOM
"WOOSH"! There were
some many sounds
everywhere. They had
killed one of his
duplicate snakes.
Not even in a minute,
all six snakes came

along to attack, but
the Undying necklace
hit them and made
them bump into the
wall. They both scream
helped until Norman
Trinity came along and
blasted each one out
of the window.

Chapter 15: The Hospital Wing

James awoke ten days later in the hospital wing, where on the right side of him stood lots of presents and Get Well Soon cards and on his left side stood Maya and Max.

"Are you alright? We heard all about the attack!" shouted the two of them.

"Yeah, my head hurts, but I'm alright. I have to tell you a secret. I have the undying necklace. That is why I survived and why I only got a couple of bruises.

"WHAT! The Leader of the magical kingdom is looking for that." Shouted the two of them

"Well, just keep it a secret.

Chapter 16: The End

Everything was normal for two months. No attacks, no mysterious people came, and George and James became friends. James even found out how to

become invisible on the
spot
And it was finally
July, so Professor
David had to tell him
the truth.

"Hello, Professor,"
said James

"Hello. It's been a
tough year, but you
made it. "

"Yep. Can you tell me that big secret?"

"Oh, I was hoping you would have forgotten. Very well, then. I am your Godfather."

"WHAT?" shouted James "I have been living in your home for a few months, and you tell me now!"

"Well, yes. I hope you
are okay."

"Yeah, I'm super
happy, though. I
finally have a father
again."

"Well here is a special
gift," said Professor
David

"Woah, It is that
action figure I have

always wanted. Thank you, Dad."

They both went back home feeling happy, but this is not the end of this story. When James was fighting the snake villain, blood dropped, and the snake took the blood. This gives him a chance to become a full body and regain all his snakes. Until the

next book, we won't
find out a thing.

Note from Author:

Thank you to all those
who bought this book.

This book is now a part
of a series called The
Adventures of James.
Hope everyone enjoys!

Many Thanks,

Hariram Suthakaran